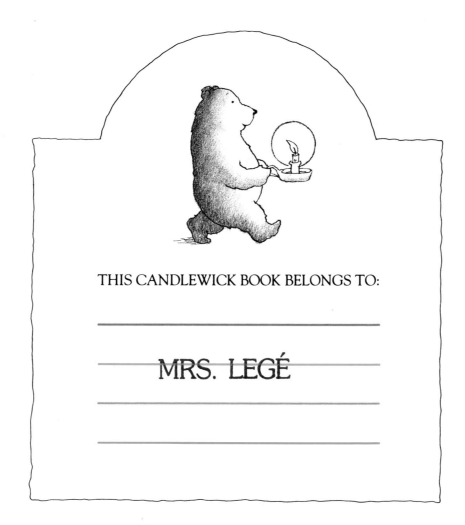

THIS CANDLEWICK BOOK BELONGS TO:

_____

MRS. LEGÉ

_____

_____

For friendships

First U.S. paperback edition 1997

The Library of Congress has cataloged the hardcover edition as follows:

Lewis, Kim.
My friend Harry / Kim Lewis.—1st U.S. ed.
Summary: A young boy takes his stuffed elephant everywhere he
goes, including on vacation and even on a visit to school.
ISBN 1-56402-617-5 (hardcover)
[1. Toys—Fiction. 2. Elephants—Fiction.] I. Title.
PZ7.L58723My   1995
[E]—dc20   94-38903

ISBN 0-7636-0285-X (paperback)

2 4 6 8 10 9 7 5 3 1

Printed in Hong Kong

This book was typeset in Plantin Educational.
The pictures were done in colored pencils.

Candlewick Press
2067 Massachusetts Avenue
Cambridge, Massachusetts 02140

My Friend Harry

Kim Lewis

CANDLEWICK PRESS
CAMBRIDGE, MASSACHUSETTS

The day James bought Harry, Harry's life changed. James talked all the way home. Harry didn't say a thing. He just sat in the car, looking clean and new and neat.

"What are you thinking?" James asked.

But Harry never said.

At the beginning of every day, when James woke up, he tossed and rumpled the blankets until Harry fell out of bed.

"Good morning, my friend Harry!" James said. "What should we do today?"

But Harry never said.

So in the mornings, James and Harry went everywhere.
They climbed to the top of the hill and back again, and
traveled from one end of the farm to the other.

In the sun and the wind and the rain, Harry's skin soon
began to wrinkle. Once he fell off James's bicycle, and
James had to fix his head.

In the afternoons James and Harry
helped his father and mother—
gathering sheep, feeding cattle, fixing
tractors, and bringing in the hay.

Both James and Harry got very
dirty. After many bathtimes
Harry's jacket shrank and
his skin began to fade.

"What are you thinking?" James asked Harry.

But Harry never said, so James hugged him tight

until Harry's ears began to flop

and his trunk began to sag.

Sometimes James made

Harry stand on his head.

Harry never complained.

"My friend Harry!"

James always said.

At the end of every day James tucked Harry into bed beside him. He read story after story and talked and talked.

"Are you listening?" He yawned. But Harry lay close to James and never said, and soon James's dad came in to kiss them.

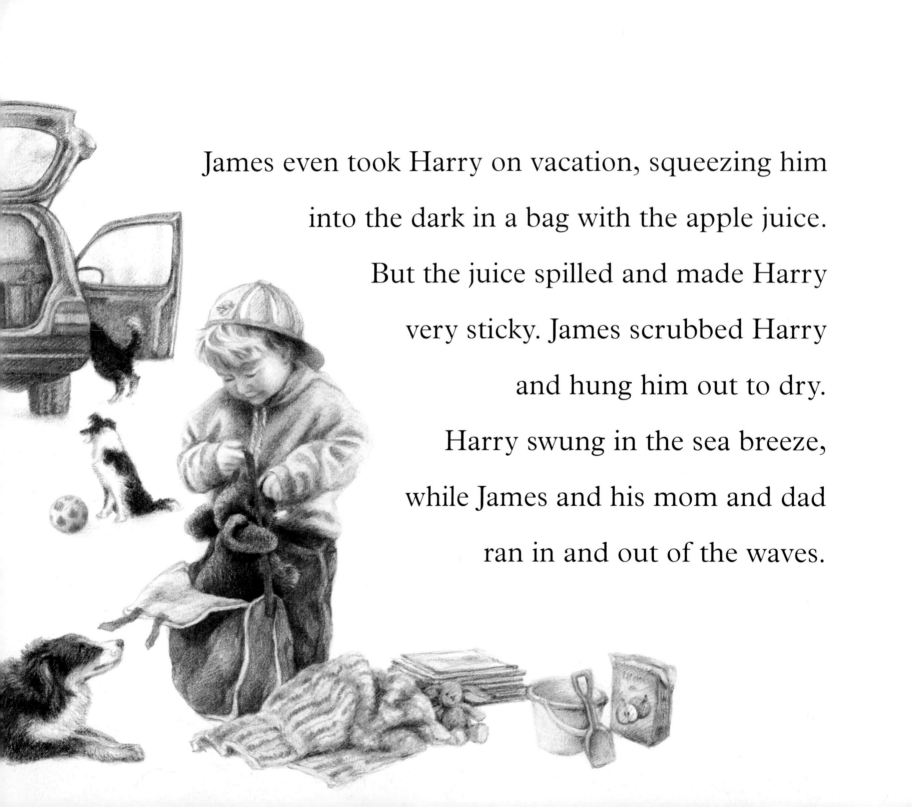

James even took Harry on vacation, squeezing him
into the dark in a bag with the apple juice.
But the juice spilled and made Harry
very sticky. James scrubbed Harry
and hung him out to dry.
Harry swung in the sea breeze,
while James and his mom and dad
ran in and out of the waves.

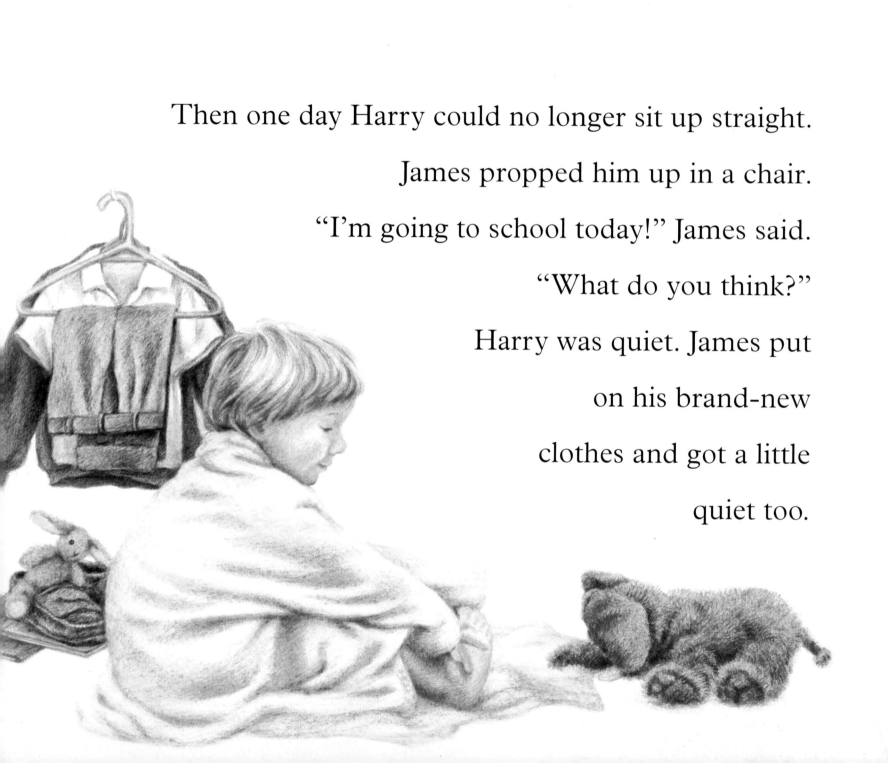

Then one day Harry could no longer sit up straight.

James propped him up in a chair.

"I'm going to school today!" James said.

"What do you think?"

Harry was quiet. James put

on his brand-new

clothes and got a little

quiet too.

Harry stayed cuddled up in James's mother's arms
while the children played all around in the school yard.
When James went into school, his mother waved,
then drove home, very quietly,
with Harry.

James's mother tucked Harry into James's bed and softly closed the door. Harry lay very still. Cows mooed faintly in the distance. James's father drove the tractor out of the yard. Birds pecked and peeped in the bushes by the house. The sun rose up and went around, warming Harry where he lay, until it was afternoon.

Harry lay still, waiting all by himself, without James.

That night, James told Harry about his day.

"I guess I'll go to school again tomorrow," he said.

Harry was very quiet.

James stared into the dark for a long time.

"Did you miss me, my friend

Harry?" he asked.

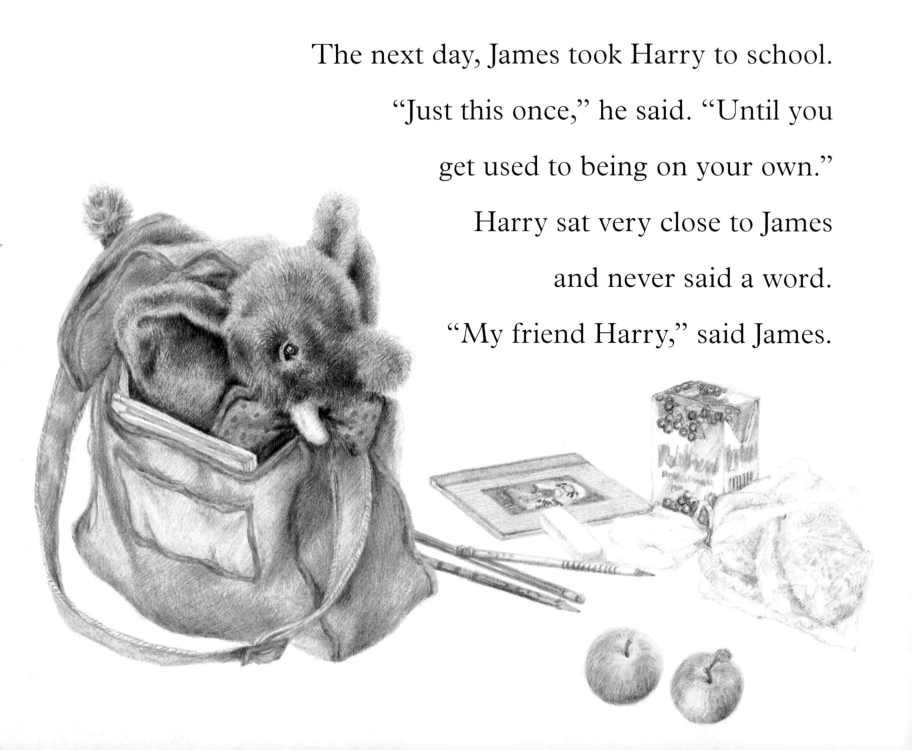

The next day, James took Harry to school.

"Just this once," he said. "Until you

get used to being on your own."

Harry sat very close to James

and never said a word.

"My friend Harry," said James.